the Star
by
Michele Breza

Copyright 2015 by Michele Breza

ISBN 978-0-9968747-0-0
Library of Congress Control Number: 2015916959

DIAMANDA
Publishing

Diamanda Publishing
Mankato, MN

A long time ago, there was a very tiny star that was destined to do great things in the Milky Way Galaxy.

It just didn't know it yet.

Night after night, as a solitary star
it pondered its existence.

It wondered why it was not part
of the Little Dipper.

The tiny star always admired Orion and was disappointed that it was not part of Orion's Belt.

5

The tiny star dreamed to shine
in the night sky as bright as the North Star.

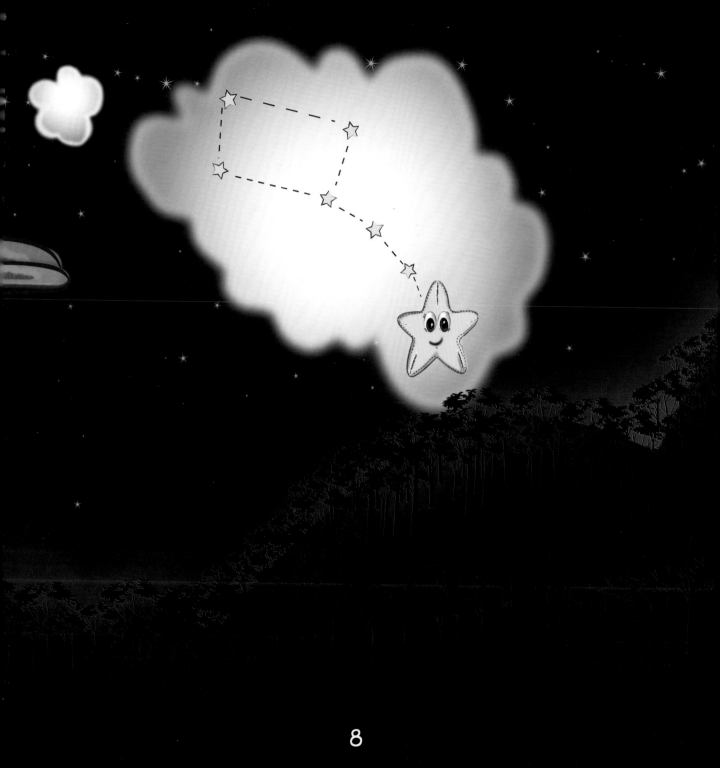

It yearned for a name
as great as the Big Dipper.

One night, the tiny star
noticed itself growing
brighter and brighter.

The star began to glide across the sky
like a shooting star.

As it moved over the ocean waters,
its reflection danced across the ebbing tide.

15

The creatures of the night looked in awe as the star soared over the countryside.

Hovering over a little town on the hillside,
the beams of light from its tips radiated
to the earth like a meteor shower.

In the silence of the night,
a soft cry from a newborn baby
echoed within the hills.

Twinkling and twirling
and dancing in the night sky,
the star discovered its purpose.

It was to announce the
Good News that Jesus was born!

the Star of Bethlehem

More illustrious than the Big Dipper,
Brighter than the North Star,
and legendary like Orion,
This once tiny star was now --
The Star of Bethlehem!

26

I was a tiny Star --
that was destined to shine above a little Town --
to announce the birth of a special Baby --
that would wear a heavenly Crown!

"The Star of Bethlehem"

This book is dedicated to my daughter, Chelsea, and my best friend, Lisa --
They continually provide support and words of wisdom when I need direction,
A listening ear when I need to throw out ideas from my ever-thinking mind,
my foundation to encourage me to dream,
and my cheerleaders to get me to the finish line.

To my parents, who eternally shine in the heavens above --
They continue to be my "guiding stars"!

Thank you to the group of illustrators and graphic designers who collaborated with
their talents to provide vivid and engaging illustrations --
Katherine De Caires,
Lindsey Hoffmann,
Cassandra Mulder,
Monica Zrust

Thank you for the insight and direction from these inspiring people who helped me
bring the book to completion:
Gale Bigbee,
Randy Kroenke,
Kevin McLaughlin,
and
the wonderful staff at Corporate Graphics.

As we each journey in self-discovery towards our divine destiny,
may we celebrate the birth of Baby Jesus every day -- not just at Christmas!

-Michele Breza